Love You Forever
Lilliana

by Suzanne
Marshall

LiveWellMedia.com

ISBN-13: 978-1544728322
ISBN-10: 1544728328

This book is dedicated to

LILLIANA

who is loved very much!

Lilliana,
when you're hurt
or feeling sick,
my love for you
will never quit.

Lilliana,
when you're feeling nervous or afraid,
I might not know just what to say...

But I'll love you more than ever.
Moods may change like weather,
but my love will last forever.

Lilliana,
when you're as silly as a circus show,
I might not always get your jokes,
but my love for you will grow and grow.

When you're feeling mad,
Lilliana,
or out of tune,
I might dream
of vacationing
on the moon...

But I'll love you more than ever.
Moods may change like weather,
but my love will last forever.

When you're feeling sad,
Lilliana,
down or blue,
never doubt my love for you.

When you're upset,
Lilliana,
that you didn't get your way,
I might dream of a
fairy-tale holiday...

But I'll love you more than ever.
Moods may change like weather,
but my love will last forever.

When you feel
embarrassed,
Lilliana,
timid or shy...

Or you're surprised
and your eyes grow wide,
I might not always understand why...

But I'll love you more than ever,
Lilliana.
Moods may change like weather,
but my love will last forever.

When you're feeling calm,
Lilliana...

Or cheerful
and carefree...

Or happy as can be...
I will love you,
Lilliana,
joyfully!

Moods may change like weather,
but my love will last forever.

When you feel
affectionate,
Lilliana,
and full of love...

I'll be ready
with a great,
big hug.

When you're feeling tired,
Lilliana,
and we say goodnight,
my love will shine
strong and bright.

Lilliana,
I love you more than ever.
Moods may change like weather,
but my love will last forever.

Special Thanks

to Mom and Dad for their love and support, and to my awesome editorial team: Rachel and Hannah Roeder, and Don Marshall. Illustrations have been edited by the author. Original pig © bolsunova, fotosearch.com. Most original scenes © colematt, fotosearch.com. Additional artwork curated from freekpik.com.

About the Author

An honors graduate of Smith College, Suzanne Marshall writes to inspire, engage and empower children. Her children's books are full of positive affirmations and inspirational quotes. Learn more about her books at: LiveWellMedia.com.

Made in the USA
Las Vegas, NV
22 March 2022